Niccolini's Song

Chuck Wilcoxen

ILLUSTRATED BY

Mark Buehner

DUTTON CHILDREN'S BOOKS : NEW YORK

A long time ago, before there were space shuttles, super-highways, or jumbo jets, there were trains.

The great engines would rest at night in rail yards, protected in the dark by watchmen.

Niccolini was a watchman.

Some watchmen were as cold and hard and strong as the engines they cared for. Niccolini was not. He was a quiet man. His wife always said he was a good listener.

Every night, dark or starry,
Niccolini would wander around
the rail yard, lantern in hand,
listening for trouble.

He hoped he wouldn't find any.

One night, Niccolini thought he heard footsteps. Well, he knew he heard footsteps, but he tried to convince himself that he hadn't.

Like all rail-yard watchmen, Niccolini had been trained in the proper use of a Hempstead Harmonic Alarm Whistle. He blew and blew.

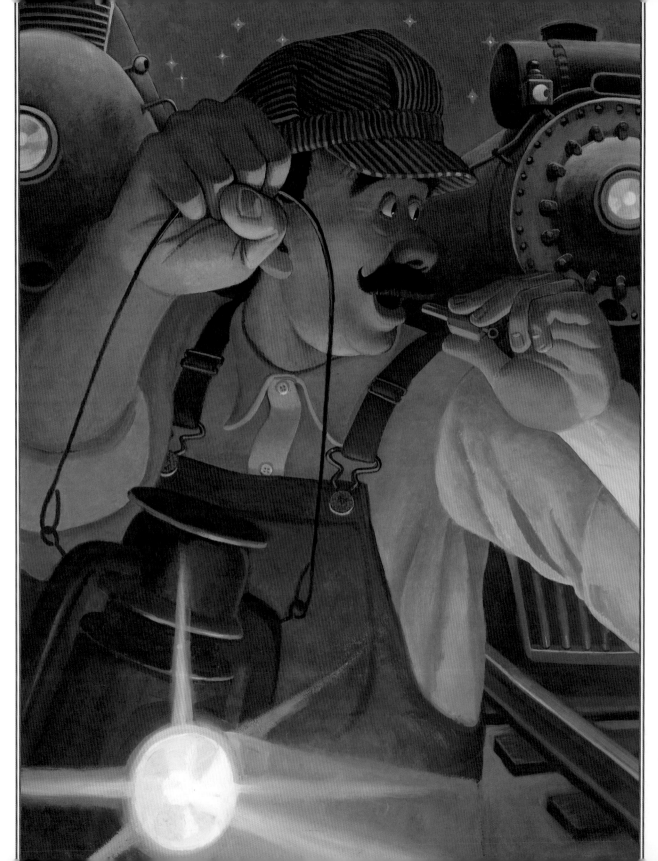

Dizzy from blowing, he stopped and listened as the footsteps raced off through the gravel, followed by panicky rattles and clanks at the fence.

On the weakest of knees, Niccolini climbed between two cars and aimed his lantern at the dark figures wobbling at the top of the fence.

Never had raccoons looked so
embarrassed or a watchman so
relieved.

Niccolini sat down next to a steam engine to collect himself. He was still just a little upset.

The night was once again quiet. Niccolini closed his eyes. A deep voice nearby whispered, "Are they gone?"

Niccolini kept his eyes closed and slowly reached for his whistle.

"No, please. No more whistling." The voice was very polite.

Niccolini opened one eye and peered to his left. He opened his other eye and peered to his right. He was certain that he was alone.

"I've got a big day tomorrow, and I'm afraid I might never get back to sleep," the voice said.

Niccolini turned to the steam engine and tilted his head.

Now, just about anybody can hear a steam engine as it thunders down the track, but it takes a very good listener to hear a steam engine worry.

"Seventy-seven boxcars from here to Waxahachie, and only three hours' sleep," it said. "Oh, oh, oh... that can't be good."

Niccolini blinked.

"Would you sing to me?" the locomotive asked. "Something low and sweet?"

Niccolini slowly turned all the way around to be absolutely sure no one was playing a trick on him. He took a step closer to the engine.

He placed his hand on the cool steel and began to hum a tune his mother used to sing to him when he was a little boy.

He could remember only some of the words, so as he began to sing, he made up a new song for the locomotive. It was a song about gentle hills, steady tail-winds, and feathers for freight.

Soon Niccolini knew the anxious engine was asleep.

The next night, Niccolini had to sing another engine to sleep, and then another and another, each with its own song.

Niccolini knew that some of the trains were perfectly capable of falling asleep without a lullaby. In fact, there were nights when certain engines (who felt unloved) would wake themselves up just to have Niccolini sing them back to sleep. Niccolini didn't mind. The words came to him easily, the tune was always the same, and it cost him nothing to bring them comfort.

One hot night, Niccolini sat at the edge of the yard, between a frustrated brake car and the wooden fence. He sang softly of smooth stops and cooperative cabooses.

On the other side of the fence, a path had been worn through the weeds by a mother who, on restless nights, would walk from the city with her baby.

She would walk and walk and walk, swaying and praying that her baby would fall asleep in her strong, soft arms.

As Niccolini sang to the brake car, he heard footsteps coming down the path. It was the mother with her baby, and this night, Niccolini was close enough to the fence for them to be caught and held by his soothing voice.

The brake car snored gently on its siding. Niccolini sang the softest, sweetest song about cool sheets and leafy breezes. The baby fell asleep. The mother whispered a thousand thanks and tiptoed back to the city.

Night after night, she would return with her baby. Niccolini would sing to them, and she would whisper her thanks over the fence.

The mother told her friends about the rail-yard lullabies, and soon there was a line of crying babies and exhausted mothers waiting at the fence for Niccolini.

The trains didn't seem to mind.

And then came the big night.

It was only wind. But it was a wind that whistled in chimneys and shook last year's kites out of the trees. Windows rattled and shutters clattered, and nobody could get to sleep.

Finally the wind quieted down. But the children in the city didn't. Babies wailed, older children tossed and turned, and parents sat on their rumpled beds, staring up at the ceiling.

Then, starting with the most desperate mothers, someone in each building remembered Niccolini.

Before too long, the rail yard was completely surrounded by crying babies, temper-troubled children, exasperated parents, and several disconcerted dogs with no other hope than Niccolini.

The noise was deafening, and the confusion was overwhelming.

Niccolini stood on a box in the middle of the yard and sang a beautiful lullaby about calm water, warm sand, deep shadows, and gently swaying hammocks.

Nobody heard a word. The crowd
was too big and murmurous.

Niccolini listened.

He walked over to a steam engine,
and it spoke to him softly.

Niccolini smiled and nodded.

He walked over to his box, climbed up, and raised his hands over his head. He pointed to the largest locomotive, and it began to blow its whistle low and soft, as if it were miles away. He pointed to a smaller engine, and it began to blow. He pointed to another, and another, and soon they were all blowing softly.

Then Niccolini began to move his hands gracefully. The whistles began to play a tune, the same tune Niccolini remembered from his childhood, the same tune the trains had heard and loved.

The crowds grew quiet. The dogs curled up and closed their red-rimmed eyes with heavy sighs. The children became calm. Babies fell asleep.

One by one, parents began
to back away from the fence,
stroking the damp hair of their
sleeping children as they quietly
carried them up the dirt path
back to the city.

One by one, Niccolini thanked each of the locomotives. One by one, they said, "You're welcome."

Niccolini picked up his lantern and listened. All he could hear was crickets and yawns.

Then all of the trains whispered together in the dark and tender night...

"Good night, Niccolini, good night."

For Gramps, who sang of Niccolini,
for Mom, who always clapped,
and for two little boys,
who always love to hear a story
C.W.

To Cara
M.B.

Library of Congress Cataloging-in-Publication Data
Wilcoxen, Chuck.
Niccolini's song / by Chuck Wilcoxen; illustrated by Mark Buehner—1st ed.
p. cm.
Summary: A gentle night watchman at the railroad yard lulls anxious train
engines to sleep by singing just the right song.
ISBN 0-525-46805-6
[1. Railroads—Trains—Fiction. 2. Lullabies—Fiction. 3. Bedtime—Fiction.]
I. Buehner, Mark, ill. II. Title.
PZ7.W645717Ni 2004
[E]—dc22 2003049250

Published in the United States 2004 by Dutton Children's Books,
a division of Penguin Young Readers Group
345 Hudson Street, New York, New York 10014
www.penguin.com
Designed by Sara Reynolds
Printed in USA • First Edition
1 2 3 4 5 6 7 8 9 10